DOROTHY HOLE

THE MARINES AND YOU

CRESTWOOD HOUSE
NEW YORK
MAXWELL MACMILLAN CANADA
TORONTO
MAXWELL MACMILLAN INTERNATIONAL
NEW YORK • OXFORD • SINGAPORE • SYDNEY

ACKNOWLEDGMENTS

Many thanks to Terry L. Bush, Sergeant, United States Marine Corps

DEDICATION

*For my sister, Margaret Field-Norbeck, who as an American Red Cross worker
served with the marines in the Pacific during World War II*

PHOTO CREDITS: *All photos courtesy of United States Marine Corps.*

Cover design, text design and production: William E. Frost Associates Ltd.

Library of Congress Cataloging-in-Publication Data

Hole, Dorothy.
    The marines and you / by Dorothy Hole. —1st ed.
      p. cm. — (The armed forces)
    Summary: Discusses life in the United States Marines, how
to join this branch of the armed forces, and how to prepare
for a future career while still serving.
    ISBN 0-89686-768-4
    1. United States. Marine Corps — Vocational guidance —
Juvenile literature. [1. United States. Marine Corps —
Vocational guidance. 2. Vocational guidance.] I. Title.
II. Series: Hole, Dorothy. Armed forces.
VE23.A13H67 1993
359.9'6'02373 — dc20   92-9771

CRESTWOOD HOUSE
MACMILLAN PUBLISHING COMPANY
866 Third Avenue
New York, NY 10022

MAXWELL MACMILLAN CANADA, INC.
1200 Eglinton Avenue East
Suite 200
Don Mills, Ontario M3C 3N1

*Macmillan Publishing Company is part of the
Maxwell Communication Group of Companies.
First Edition
Printed in the United States of America*

10 9 8 7 6 5 4 3 2 1

CONTENTS

This amphibious tractor crew is trained to fight to protect the interests of the United States both on land and in the water.

CHAPTER ONE

WHAT IS A MARINE?

Ever since you were a kid, you've known the tune. "From the halls of Montezuma," you sing loud and strong, "to the shores of Tripoli." Those are the words to "The Marines' Hymn." Okay, so you don't know where those places are, but you guess the marines were there once upon a time.

Just what are the marines? You probably know that the United States Marine Corps is one of the armed services. There are also the army, navy, air force and Coast Guard. From their names you know what they do. Where do the marines fit in?

A marine is a seagoing soldier, serving on ships as well as on land. The Marine Corps is an **amphibious** fighting force.

Amphibious refers to something that lives on both land and in the water. A frog is amphibious; so is a crocodile.

The Marine Corps also has aviation units. As an enlisted **leatherneck**, you cannot be a pilot. If you are interested in flying, you might become an airborne radio operator. Then you fly as a member of an enlisted flight crew. All marine aviation personnel are fully skilled ground marines as well. You all go through **basic training** together.

Sounds pretty good. Before you decide to enlist, however, you should find out more about the day-to-day life of a marine. Ask yourself some important questions, such as, "How do I react to pressure? Do I lose my cool or get on with my job? Do I do a slow burn when ordered to do something I don't want to do? What about discipline? Can I take it or does my anger flare up? Can I control my temper? How about being on a ship for long periods? Would being away from home for six months upset me? Would I be homesick living in a foreign country?"

Perhaps the most important question to consider is the part the Marine Corps plays in an armed conflict. Marines have fought in every war the United States has had since the Corps began way back in 1775. They've had to fight in such faraway places as China and North Africa even when the United States was *not* at war.

All marines serve "at the pleasure of the president." This means the president can send members of the Corps wherever and whenever he believes United States citizens and American interests are in danger.

That explains the list of invasions of foreign lands by marines when the United States was not at war. They were in Nicaragua from 1926 until 1933. They landed in the Dominican Republic in 1965. After a two-year stay, they pulled out of Lebanon in 1984.

As a marine, you never know where you'll be sent next.

Teamwork is essential to marine strategy. Be sure that you are able to work well with others before you decide to enlist.

Interested in seeing what lies below the water's surface? As a member of the marines, you may learn to scuba dive.

The marines form expeditionary units that come from ships to lead assaults on enemy territory. Their planes give support to the ground forces. The marines are in the thick of fighting. Is that where you want to be? How do you react to danger?

About 15 percent of the marines are routinely assigned aboard navy ships, either as part of the ship's company (sea duty) or as an attached Marine Expeditionary Unit (MEU). They have other duties as well. Marines guard the president on his visits to Camp David. They do security duty at United States embassies around the world.

"Navy?" you ask.

Although it has its own commanding four-star general, the Marine Corps is under the Department of the Navy. The marines need the navy for transportation. To land successfully on enemy territory, the marines must have the navy's cooperation.

During peacetime some marines are assigned sea duty to provide security aboard larger navy ships, such as aircraft carriers and command ships.

It would be great if you could be a marine only during peacetime. Unfortunately, conflicts burst unexpectedly. It's something to think about.

Is the Marine Corps right for you? Only you can answer. Perhaps your school counselor can help. The counselor knows you better than you realize. Your records show what your teachers think of you. They know if you misbehave in class, if you're a troublemaker, if you're on drugs or alcohol.

Your counselor can only advise. It's up to *you* and *you alone* to make the decision. After all, it's your life.

Marine Corps soldiers are well-trained, disciplined men and women who must be prepared to be called on during national emergencies.

CHAPTER TWO

FIRST STEP: THE ASVAB

First of all, as your counselor will tell you, you must take a test, the **Armed Services Vocational Aptitude Battery (ASVAB)**. This is a must for everyone wanting to enlist in any of the armed services. In fact, the enlistment process is the same for all of them.

The Marine Corps wants to know what skills you have, what subjects you do best in, what interests you the most. Only by learning about *you* can the Corps assign you to a job that you like and can do successfully. Of course, there must be an opening in that job skill before you can be assigned to it. (More about that later.)

The ASVAB is one of the ways the Corps uses to discover what abilities you have. This test is given at high schools. If your school doesn't give it, a marine **recruiter** can arrange for you to take it at another school.

You can study for it, just as you can for any exam. Check out the books on the ASVAB from the library. Don't rush through the sample tests. Use them to learn which subjects are your weak ones and which are your strong ones. Use this knowledge to guide you in the work you choose. Knowing the sort of questions you will have to answer makes taking the real ASVAB easier.

The subjects you'll be quizzed about range from electronics, mathematics and auto and shop information to general science and word knowledge.

Try this sample math problem:

"If 50 percent of X = 66, then X =

    A. 33

    B. 132

    C. 99

    D. 66"

Know which is correct?

From the recruiter find out your score and what it means. Some schools invite a recruiter to discuss scoring with the students. This is important even if you decide not to enlist in the marines. It gives you an idea of what sort of jobs you should apply for in civilian life. You may be surprised.

Do your best. Don't let worrying about failing upset you. The Marine Corps doesn't expect you to know everything. If you don't pass, you can retake the exam after 30 days have gone by. You then have another chance after six months to try again.

With the ASVAB over, you now want more facts about the Corps. There's one place to go: a marine recruiting station. You'll find it listed in the telephone book under "United States Government, Marine Corps Recruiting."

Although the majority of soldiers are men, women are permitted to serve in many positions in the United States Marine Corps.

When you reach the recruiting station, you ask the recruiter, "Why is a marine called a leatherneck?"

The recruiter tells you that the nickname comes from the first uniforms the marines wore. Back in the 1700s their uniforms had a high collar. It was like a stiff turtleneck made of leather. It did not fold over. This high leather collar protected a marine's neck in hand-to-hand fighting. They became known as leathernecks. And the nickname has stuck for over 200 years!

You debate whether or not to enlist. If you decide to, will the Corps accept you?

The recruiter cannot promise. You must qualify. Both men and women serve in the Corps and the same requirements hold for both sexes, except on the ASVAB. Women are required to score higher because the Marine Corps needs fewer women.

From age 17 through age 28, you are eligible to join, providing you meet other standards. Between your 17th and

Some Marine Corps recruits are stationed on land while others may be stationed aboard ships.

your 18th birthdays, you must have the consent of your parent or guardian. If you are a single parent, the sole custody of a child will disqualify you.

There are certain legal papers you need:

1. Birth certificate, social security card, or other proof of citizenship
2. Proof of citizenship if you were born out of the country and your parents are U.S. citizens
3. Proof of legal entry for permanent residency (green card) if you were born out of the country and your parents are *not* United States citizens

In order to enlist, you are required to have a high school diploma or a GED and 15 units of college credits. The Corps urges you to complete your high school education before enlisting.

You are given a physical exam and checked to make sure you are not a security risk to the United States government.

You may enlist for three, four, five or six years. For some jobs, the Corps offers you an enlistment **bonus**. That bonus can go up to $5,000. Before signing on for a job that gives you a bonus, think it over carefully. Accepting an enlistment bonus may entail a longer enlistment contract.

In actual fact, you will be signing up for eight years. You spend the difference between your **active service** and the end of your enlistment period in the Marine Corps Reserve. You have no duties during this time. However, you can be called into active service in an emergency.

United States Marine Corps bands are famous for their music as well as for their marching precision.

CHAPTER THREE

WHY JOIN THE MARINES?

Among the benefits involved in being a marine are a steady paycheck, a 30-day paid vacation each year, free medical and dental care and free housing. Unless you're assigned to a ship, you live on the base if there is a vacancy. If not, then you live off the base and receive a housing allowance to cover additional off-the-base living expenses.

On most bases you find a movie theater, library, swimming pool, tennis court, gym and other recreational facilities. You shop at the **commissary** (supermarket) and the **post exchange** (department store). Prices are lower at these government-owned stores than in commercial enterprises.

At some time you may be stationed out of the country. You actually live in a foreign country and visit places that were only names on a map to you before you joined the marines. Even overseas you don't have to worry about becoming ill. Your free medical and dental plans take care of the expense. And if you're stationed aboard a ship, you still have free entertainment—movies and closed circuit TV as well as libraries and gyms.

The Corps is anxious for you to continue your education. Both men and women are urged to keep on studying. You can enroll in one of the various programs the marines offer. An education officer, attached to each major command, will help

Women in the Marine Corps are now being trained in many of the same disciplines as men.

you figure out what courses to take and how to apply for tuition (money charged for taking a course).

"I'm finished with studying," you announce. "I want action, not books!" In a year or two you may change your mind. Better find out about it now while you're talking to the recruiter.

One of the most significant benefits that you receive is expert training in whichever job skill you choose. If you decide not to reenlist, this will give you an advantage in the civilian job market. Or if you serve 20 years and then retire, you have even more experience and that makes you even more valuable to an employer.

The Corps attempts to match you, your skills and your interests to the vacancies that exist in the Corps. This is done with the help of a computer that is kept up-to-date about openings in the various marine occupations.

There are so many job options for you in the marines, it makes your head whirl! Some jobs are limited to men. However, with the passing of a new law by the Congress in the summer of 1991, women may now serve in combat zones although not in offensive roles. However, a Department of Defense commission has been established to analyze and recommend future combat roles for women.

The Marine Corps is divided into 41 occupational fields. Each of these areas has a variety of choices. When you choose an occupational field, you are not guaranteed which particular skill you will be doing in that field. Take aircraft maintenance. There are many options, including aviation maintenance administration and three specialties under aviation support equipment technician (mechanical, hydraulic and electrical). Which job you do is determined by the needs of the Marine Corps.

In other words, you might pick engineer, construction and equipment (Field #13) because you want to be a combat

engineer. If the Corps needs basic metalworkers (which is in the same field), you'll be a basic metalworker.

As you can see, there are many advantages in joining the marines. There are also many disadvantages: You may feel you are trapped, that you have no freedom to make decisions about where you live, where you go, about changing to another job when you feel like it—you just can't quit and walk away. When you sign the enlistment contract, you are committing yourself for a definite period of time. It is possible to request a transfer from one specialty area to another; however, this request may be denied. Enlisting in the marines is not something you rush into.

Things that annoy you may be small, but sometimes the small irritations can ruin your day, your work or your life. Once the contract is signed, you cannot change your mind until your enlistment is up. Then if you're unhappy, you don't reenlist.

You can change your job skill after various lengths of time. However, you have to move laterally from one specialty area to another. That means you cannot be assigned to a job at a lower rank than you hold at that moment.

True, some people love being a marine. They reenlist time and again. They enjoy the friendships that bond marines throughout the world. They are proud of their Corps and proud to wear the marine uniform.

If you decide to enlist, the recruiter will ask you to fill out an application form. This form asks questions about your parents and your background. Signing an application does *not* mean you are in the marines.

You must go through a **Military Entrance Processing Station (MEPS)** first.

(Photo left) By the time your enlistment period is up, you will probably have received enough training in your occupational specialty to be considered an expert in the field.

All Marine Corps recruits are required to go through a 12-week basic training period at the start of their enlistment.

CHAPTER FOUR

THE DAY THAT CHANGES YOUR LIFE

This may be the day that changes your life.

At the MEPS you find out if you qualify for the Marine Corps. You have important decisions to make. Do you really want to be a marine? What type of work do you want to do? These two questions alone can decide your future.

The day begins early. You must report to the MEPS between 5:30 A.M. and 6:30 A.M. If you are unable to get there on time, the Marine Corps arranges transportation. You may live so far from the MEPS that the Corps provides a free hotel room before and a free breakfast that morning.

Before you check into the hotel, you need a signed authorization from your recruiter, a valid ID and a MEPS form signed by your recruiter.

You must be in your hotel room by 10:00 P.M. You begin to get a taste of marine life when a bed check is made. You are awakened at 3:30 A.M. (the middle of the night!) as you must be ready for breakfast by 4:00 A.M. and to leave for the MEPS an hour later.

If you haven't taken the ASVAB, you will take the exam today. It's risky to wait until now. There are so many other things going on at this time, it may be hard for you to concentrate.

Usually the first event is your physical. This is done by a Department of Defense doctor. You will be tested for HIV, the virus that causes AIDS. Your eyes will be examined. Bring along your glasses and contact lenses, if you wear them.

The doctor wants to know of any medicine your own doctor has prescribed. If possible, bring along a copy of your health record from your family doctor.

Tell the examining doctor of any operations or serious illness you have had. Your blood alcohol level is tested. Any alcohol abuse problems may show up here. You will not become a marine if you test positive for drugs.

Next you go to the **Entrance National Agency Checks (ENTNAC)**. What they check on is you. Are you a security risk to the United States? Probably not, but the marines have to be sure. You are fingerprinted. The FBI keeps a copy of your fingerprints with your records. Your application form is reviewed to be sure you have answered all the questions.

By now you're getting hungry. Lunch is free if you eat in the MEPS dining room. If you eat at a restaurant outside the MEPS building, you have to pay for it yourself.

After lunch you have the interview that changes your life. What job will you do in the marines? A marine guidance counselor looks at the results of your ASVAB and discusses

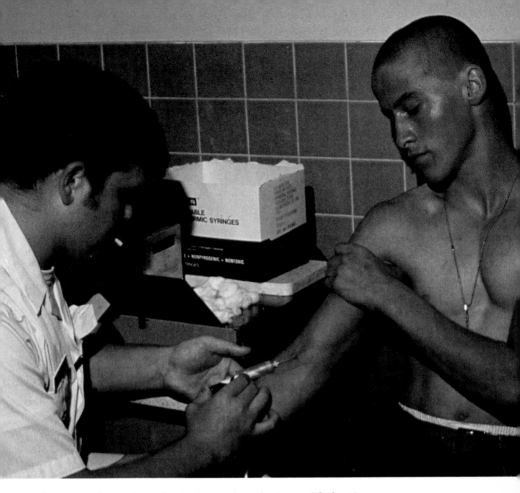

Be prepared to take a physical exam in order to qualify for the Marine Corps.

your interests with you. The counselor then uses a computer to match your job choice, the needs of the Marine Corps and the openings in the Corps.

You may find you qualify for work you never thought about. What about weather? As a member of the Weather Service, you must give accurate forecasts. A squadron may take to the air or be grounded by your findings. Lives depend on what you report.

How about amphibian tractor crewman? You must be a man for this job, although that may change. As an assault amphibian crewman, you'll be right in the center of the action. Maybe you deliver infantrymen from ship to beach. Maybe you operate a two-way radio, keeping communications open during a landing.

You might become a combat engineer. Your experience operating heavy machinery, building roads and welding are all skills that can help you in the civilian job market.

Do you play a musical instrument? Marine bands are famous not only for their music—some of the best in the world—but also for their marching precision. An enlisted musician attends **recruit** training like all other new marines.

You're disappointed. There is no opening in the job field you want. *Don't* change your choice. Being unhappy with what you do can make you miserable. If there is no vacancy in, say, electronics maintenance, do not enlist in legal services just because there is a place open there.

The marines have the answer: the **Delayed Entry Program (DEP)**. You don't report for active duty right away. The DEP has two purposes. One is to allow the enlistee the opportunity to receive the job field he or she wants. The other is to allow a young man or woman to complete his or her senior year of high school before entering the Marine Corps.

Perhaps you qualify to enter under the **Quality Enlistment Program (QEP)**. This is mainly for men and women who hope to make the Corps their career. They receive an increase in salary and have a choice of location for their first duty station. Ask about it.

There's another program, called the **College Enlistment Program (CEP)**. If you attend a community college or a vocational or technical school, you may qualify. Faster promo-

26

There are many jobs and skills needed to run the United States Marine Corps. This soldier has received training in the field of communications.

tions and guarantees that you will remain in the job skill you picked are some of the benefits.

Discuss all of these options with the marine career guidance counselor at the MEPS. The counselor is a professional there to help you.

After reviewing your choices, you decide the job field you want to be in.

All that remains to be done is to have your picture taken and for you to pledge the oath that makes you a marine.

In boot camp you will learn everything you need to know about your M-16A2 rifle.

CHAPTER FIVE

BOOT CAMP

You're eager to start your marine career. You want to leave that same day. Don't be disappointed, but that's not the way it's usually done. A few days or weeks later, you report to the MEPS. You and all the other new enlistees are bused or flown to your training camps.

Men and women undergo the same intense 12-week training. If you're a woman, you head for Parris Island, South Carolina. Men go to either Parris Island or San Diego, California.

You may arrive late in the day or at night. You're tired, excited and, at the same time, a little frightened. You feel weird, lying on your bunk, surrounded by strangers. Nothing is familiar. You had to leave almost all your possessions at home—even your car. It's a shock, suddenly finding yourself in the **barracks**. Everything is different from your civilian life. You begin to have doubts. Maybe joining the marines was a wrong move.

Don't worry—each of the new enlistees is having the same thoughts you are. Adjusting to military life can be tough. Before long your barracks-mates are your best friends. More importantly, you act as a team. But that first night you wonder if that will really happen.

Before you begin actual training, there are some matters to be taken care of, such as your hair. Women's hair is worn in most any style as long as it is neat, allows the woman to wear her hat properly and the length clears the collar of her uniform. Men's hair is cut so short they don't need a comb!

The main purpose of basic training is to teach new marines how to survive during combat situations.

You are assigned to your barracks (your home away from home). Within 72 hours of arriving, you are issued your uniform. Your civilian clothes and personal belongings are sent home. Along with your uniform, you receive underwear, boots, cartridge belt, first aid kit, bedding and blankets.

You also receive your most important possession: your rifle. Don't make the mistake of calling it a gun! Never even think of it as a gun! Your "piece" is all right; your "rifle" is okay. You learn to strip it; that is, to take it apart for cleaning and adjustment, and then put it together again.

It's an M-16A2 rifle, which is so vital to a marine that there is a creed that each marine repeats. In it you say, "My rifle is my best friend. It is my life....My rifle without me is useless. Without my rifle, I am useless....I will keep my rifle clean and ready even as I am clean and ready....My rifle and I are the defenders of my country."

With 70 other new arrivals, you are assigned to a recruit **platoon**. You hear a welcoming talk from an **officer** who explains what you may and may not do. Then you meet your **senior drill instructor**, your **DI**.

It's the DI's job to teach you how to survive under combat. It's not easy for the DI, and it's definitely not easy for you. The DI drives you so hard you feel that you can't stand up another moment—and then yells, "Twenty more push-ups!" The DI puts you through more gymnastics than an Olympic hopeful. You load yourself with your rifle, helmet, cartridge belt and shovel, and then you're ordered to grab a rope, swing over a river and drop to the ground on the other side. You leap over water-filled barriers. You march close-order drill. You learn judo, hand-to-hand combat movements and the use of the bayonet.

And when the DI shouts an order, you do it! Right then! No questions asked! Don't *ever* get on the wrong side of your DI.

31

New recruits must endure an intense physical conditioning program in order to meet the requirements of basic training.

Man or woman, the DI can make your life miserable. And no, he or she isn't picking on you. It just seems that way.

Remember, the DI has a terrific responsibility. A saying of DIs proclaims, "Let's be damn sure that no man's ghost will ever say, 'If your training program had only done its job.'"

Under combat you'll be grateful to your DI. What he or she teaches you now will save your life then.

There's more to **boot camp** than physical workouts. There are classroom courses as well. Among the subjects you study are military sanitation; personal hygiene; guard duty; rights and privileges of a member of the armed services and of an American citizen; first aid; marine customs, courtesy and traditions; and the history of the Marine Corps.

You learn that on November 10, 1775, the Continental Congress voted that "two battalions of marines be raised." These first marines were skilled riflemen who were trained to pick off enemy sailors during battles between warships on the seas. Twenty-three years later the Marine Corps became part of the navy, which it still is today.

At last you discover the answers to the "halls of Montezuma" and the "shores of Tripoli." Where are they and why do the marines sing about them? Montezuma's halls refers to the National Palace in Mexico that was captured by marines during the Mexican War.

Tripoli is the capital of Libya. Back in the early 1800s, pirates from Tripoli on the North African Barbary Coast raided ships sailing on the Mediterranean Sea. They captured sailors and interrupted trading. The marines played a large part in destroying the pirates. The ruler of Tripoli gave a copy of a Mameluke sword to a young marine lieutenant, Presley O'Bannon. Today a copy of that sword is carried by marine officers on dress occasions.

Upholding the traditions of the Marine Corps is an awesome challenge.

Basic Training Graduation Day is a proud one indeed for new Marine Corps soldiers and their families.

CHAPTER SIX

BECOMING AN EXPERT

When you realize how much you've learned in 12 weeks, it seems unbelievable. You now know how to shoot a rifle by using the correct position, adjusting the sling and the sights, squeezing the trigger—"snapping in," as it's called. You must also know about a .45 caliber pistol. Not all marines carry one, but you need to know how to use it.

You've learned to swim carrying equipment, successfully finish an obstacle course and pitch a tent so that rain and mosquitoes can't get in. You're in better physical shape than you've ever been.

Now you march proudly with your platoon on graduation day. Basic training is over.

All marines are given at least ten days of vacation after recruit graduation. These ten days are part of the 30 days of annual leave every marine gets each year. After their leave, men go to **Marine Combat Training (MCT)** and women go directly to training in their career choice **(formal schooling)**.

At MCT, you go on **maneuvers**—living under combat conditions. You attack (pretend) enemy positions. You practice your combat skills and are taught how and when to use other weapons, such as a machine gun.

Perhaps the most important thing you learn is the fact that you are part of a marine rifle **squad**. The idea of working (and fighting) as a team is basic to all marine functions.

Now you are ready for specialized training in your skill, your formal schooling.

Men and women go to the same schools. Where will you go? It all depends on what field you will be working in. How long will your formal schooling last? Some lasts as little as 3 weeks (microwave equipment repair at Twenty-nine Palms, California) or as long as 45 weeks (improved Hawk missile system maintenance technician at Redstone Arsenal, Alabama).

These schools are scattered across the country. Most of them, but not all, are in California, Tennessee, Virginia, Alabama, Texas and North Carolina.

If you are interested in ordnance (ammunition, explosives), you go to Aberdeen, Maryland. To become an audio/television production specialist, you train at Lowry Technical Training Center in Colorado. An avionics (aircraft electrician) maintenance marine trains in Memphis, Tennessee. And if you want to learn how to maintain meteorological (weather) equipment, you spend 16 weeks at Chanute Air Force Base in Illinois.

An extra benefit for marines choosing a field that in civilian life has a **journeyman** status is the apprenticeship program. A record of your work—an "experience log"—is given to you. When you have finished your training and the required number of hours on the job, the Department of Labor will grant you a Certificate of Completion, making you a journeyman in that skill. Examples of journeyman skills are carpentry and printing.

As a Marine Corps soldier, you must be able to follow orders from your superiors. Discipline will be vital to your success as a leatherneck.

This is of great value when you join the civilian work force, whether that happens at the end of your active enlistment period or 20 years from now when you retire. Your future employer knows your ability has been tested by the Corps.

No matter what job you do in the marines, it is usually one that people's lives depend on. From aircraft maintenance to food supply to computer programming to weather forecasts, someone needs an expert—and you may be that marine.

CHAPTER SEVEN

THE FIGHTING MARINES

While still in boot camp, you may be one of those promoted by your commanding officer for excellent performance. However, the norm is to be promoted after six months of service. All promotions up to sergeant **(E-5)** take place only with the recommendation of your commanding officer. Beyond sergeant, you are selected at U.S. Marine Corps Headquarters, by a promotion board.

You enter the marines as a **private (E-1)** without any insignia on your sleeve. Then you advance to a **private first class (E-2)** and earn your first chevron (one patch for each sleeve).

To move from private first class to lance corporal **(E-3)** usually takes eight months time-in-grade (TIG) and nine months time-in-service (TIS). That means you can be promoted to lance corporal nine months after you enlist, providing you've been a private first class for eight of those nine months.

Marine Corps uniforms have changed over the years since the Corps was first established in 1775. The current uniform is shown here, although the insignia varies according to the soldier's rank.

To go from lance corporal to corporal **(E-4)**, you must have eight months TIG and 12 months TIS. Each rating has a different TIS and TIG.

Along with a new rank, you receive an increase in salary and a change of insignia on your sleeves. You must know which insignia stands for which rank before you finish boot camp.

What rank is a marine whose patch has two crossed rifles inside a white triangle formed by three chevrons above and two bars below? If you answered gunnery sergeant, you're right!

If you're a woman, boot camp and formal schooling in your job skill are behind you. If you're a man, MCT is as well. Now you're ready for your first **tour of duty**. That is the term used to describe the length of time you are assigned to a specific place.

You will probably be assigned to the **Fleet Marine Force (FMF)** and go to either Camp Lejeune, North Carolina, or Camp Pendleton, California. Approximately 85 percent of all marines are in the FMF.

You still eat in the **mess hall** and sleep in barracks. Married personnel live either on the base if housing is available or, if unavailable, off the base, for which they receive a housing allowance.

You are now part of a permanent unit of the Marine Corps. Your time is spent practicing and perfecting your skills in whichever career field you picked, such as **infantry**, motor transport, public affairs or data systems.

Unless you are on special duty, you knock off work at 4:30 P.M. Your free time is yours to spend as you wish. You can watch TV, take a swim or play baseball.

Twice a year you and all marines have to pass a tough **Physical Fitness Test (PFT)**. Because of that, most marines spend part of their free time in sports. Some competitions are organized, like the All-Marine Track and Field Meet. Some are informal get-togethers to play basketball or soccer. Join in. This keeps you in top physical form so you will pass the PFT without any problems.

You and your unit will take part in large-scale amphibious maneuvers. This gives you a chance to practice your skills under combat conditions.

Living on the base is like living in a small town. Everything you need is right there: post office, laundry service, stores and just about everything else you can think of.

Women cannot become seagoing marines. This is because these marines are, first and foremost, fighters who make assault landings. Women are not permitted in attack (offensive) fighting.

If you're a man ordered to **the Fleet**, you must have certain qualifications. You must have a military appearance and be precise in performing drills. Your shipboard duties include security of the brig (jail) and sentry duty.

On shipboard you bunk with the marine detachment. You eat your meals with the sailors. "We're just one big, happy family," one marine sergeant claims. This is good, because a warship's **deployment** (time away from home port) sometimes lasts for six months or more. Your time in foreign ports can be fun as you learn about other lands and people. Take lots of pictures to send back home!

Additional training prepares you for special assignments. You might be assigned to embassy duty. Or become a marine recruiter. Or a marine career counselor. For any of these, you must have been in the Corps at least four years.

If you joined the infantry, you might consider becoming a scout swimmer, commonly known as a **frogman**. You learn scuba diving. This involves slipping over the side of a rubber boat about 500 yards offshore. You might have to scout enemy positions, remove obstructions that could damage a landing craft and return safely to your ship. In war it's exciting and dangerous.

"What," you ask, "if I want to experience Marine Corps life but I don't want to do it full-time?"

The reserves were meant for you!

When you enlist in the Marine Corps, you are committing yourself to the United States armed forces for a number of years. Enlistment is not a decision that should be taken lightly. Be sure to weigh the pros and cons of Marine Corps life before you decide to become a "soldier of the sea."

CHAPTER EIGHT

SEMPER FIDELIS

Being a part-time marine interests you. You learn that the requirements are the same to become a regular or a **reservist**. Men and women must be at least 17 years old and under age 29. You must meet the citizenship requirements and pass the physical. You attend boot camp with the regulars and, if you're a man, receive the same MCT. How long you remain on active status depends on the career field you have selected. You receive regular marine pay while on active service.

If you are a high school senior graduating within six months, you are eligible to receive full pay for attending weekend drill. Marine reservists receive approximately one-half the benefits and funds for education under the **New G.I. Bill (Reserve)** as regular leathernecks. However, reserve marines are not required to enroll in the New G.I. Bill (Reserve) program to receive benefits, nor do they contribute $100 per month for 12 months, as do active-duty marines who enroll in the New G.I. Bill (Reserve) program. When your training is finished, as a reservist you take part in drills one weekend a month. You spend two weeks each year updating your training at a Marine Corps camp. You might even find yourself taking part in joint international maneuvers!

"The fighting marines!" "The marines have landed!" "Soldiers of the sea!" "Devil dogs!" All of those are affectionate ways of referring to the marines.

Don't let the glamour of the uniform, of the tradition, of the fame of the marines convince you that you should enlist. Never forget the everyday duties, not being able to make every decision about your life, being away from home, being aware that at any moment you can be ordered to take part in an assault. For every yes there is a no.

It all depends on you. You know yourself best. The Marine Corps motto, *Semper Fidelis*, means "always faithful." If you join the Marine Corps, you must be always faithful to your country. But in the Marine Corps or out, you must be always faithful to yourself.

GLOSSARY

active reserve A civilian who serves part-time in the marines but has a regular full-time job.

active service As an active service member, the marines is your only job. You are a full-time marine.

amphibious Living both on land and in the water. The marines are an amphibious armed service, as they fight and train on both.

Armed Services Vocational Aptitude Battery (ASVAB) Test required of everyone who hopes to join one of the armed services.

barracks Building in which you sleep and keep your possessions.

basic training The first instruction you receive after reporting for duty.

bonus Extra money given to those who enlist or reenlist for certain jobs, usually those that the Marine Corps has the greatest need for.

boot camp Same as basic training.

College Enlistment Program (CEP) One of the programs under which you can enlist in the marines.

commissary Supermarket operated by the government.

Delayed Entry Program (DEP) A program for putting off (delaying) your reporting for active service after you have enlisted.

deployment Time a naval ship is away from home port.

Entrance National Agency Checks (ENTNAC) The agency that checks your background to be sure you are not a security risk to the United States.

E-1, E-2, E-3, up to E-9 Pay grades. All services have the same pay grades.

the Fleet A group of naval warships under a single command.

Fleet Marine Force (FMF) Approximately 85 percent of marines are assigned to the FMF. Land and sea based, they are always at-the-ready to be called into action on a moment's notice.

formal schooling The term used for the training you receive in your job choice after finishing basic training.

frogman An infantryman who is given special training as a scout swimmer.

inactive reserve After you have finished your active service, you are in the inactive reserve for the time remaining under your enlistment contract. You are also placed in the inactive reserve while in the Delayed Entry Program.

infantry Foot soldiers. Basic transportation is by foot.

journeyman A person who has finished his or her apprenticeship and learned a craft or skill.

leatherneck Nickname for a marine.

maneuvers A practice battle or war, involving the changing of the marines' positions to give them the advantage over the enemy.

Marine Combat Training (MCT) Learning to use military equipment and to fight under battle conditions.

mess hall Dining room.

Military Entrance Processing Station (MEPS) The place where you take your physical, pass a security check, decide the kind of work you hope to do in the marines, sign the enlistment contract and take the oath.

New G.I. Bill (Reserve) A government bill that provides a way for marines to save money for college after completion of service.

noncommissioned officer (noncom) An enlisted marine from the rank of corporal (E-4) and sergeant (E-5).

officer A person who has received special training to qualify for a commission, making that person higher in rank than enlisted personnel and noncommissioned officers.

Physical Fitness Test (PFT) Tough physical exam each marine must pass twice a year.

platoon A unit of approximately 40 people.

post exchange Department store operated by the government.

private Lowest rank in the Marine Corps.

private first class One rank above a private.

Quality Enlistment Program (QEP) One of the programs under which you can enlist in the marines. This program is mainly for men and women who hope to make the Corps their career.

recruit A person who has recently joined (enlisted in) one of the armed services.

recruiter A person who enlists new people into the Marine Corps.

reservist A member of a reserve unit.

senior drill instructor (DI) The person (male or female) in charge of your basic training at boot camp.

squad The smallest unit of enlisted personnel (approximately ten marines).

tour of duty Amount of time you are assigned to a specific place.

INDEX